7/09

Library of Congress Cataloging-in-Publication Data

Callahan, Sean, 1965-
A wild Father's Day / by Sean Callahan ; illustrated by Daniel Howarth.
p. cm.
Summary: As they enjoy indoor and outdoor activities on Father's Day, a father and his children pretend to be wild animals.
ISBN 978-0-8075-2293-6
[1. Father's Day—Fiction. 2. Animals—Fiction.] I. Howarth, Daniel, ill. II. Title.
PZ7.C12974Wi 2009   [E]   dc22 2008027443

Text copyright © 2009 by Sean Callahan.
Illustrations copyright © 2009 by Daniel Howarth.
Published in 2009 by Albert Whitman & Company,
6340 Oakton Street, Morton Grove, Illinois 60053-2723.
Published simultaneously in Canada by Fitzhenry & Whiteside,
Markham, Ontario. All rights reserved. No part of this book may be reproduced
or transmitted in any form or by any means, electronic or mechanical,
including photocopying, recording, or by any information storage
and retrieval system, without permission in writing from the publisher.
Printed in China.
10 9 8 7 6 5 4 3 2 1

The design is by Carol Gildar.

For more information about Albert Whitman & Company,
please visit our web site at www.albertwhitman.com.

A Wild Father's Day

Sean Callahan

Illustrated by Daniel Howarth

Albert Whitman & Company, Morton Grove, Illinois

HA CASS COUNTY PUBLIC LIBRARY
400 E. MECHANIC
HARRISONVILLE, MO 64701

0 0022 0350005 9

For Nancy, Sophie, Charlotte, Mom, and Dad.—s.c.

To my father, as strong as a bear and as kind
as an elephant. Thank you.—d.h.

Early on Father's Day, the kids gave Daddy a
card. It said, "Have a wild Father's Day!"

Daddy wiped the sleep from his eyes and said,
"A *wild* Father's Day? I know just what to do.
Let's act like animals all day long!

"We'll hop on the bed
like kangaroos.

Boing, *boing* . . .

boing!

"We'll stretch like cats.

Streeeeeeeetch!

"We'll run fast like cheetahs.

Zip, zip . . .

"We'll swing like monkeys.

Chee, chee . . .

chee!

"We'll wrestle like bears.

Grapple, grapple, grapple!

"We'll swim like dolphins.

"We'll eat special Father's Day cookies, the way elephants eat peanuts.

"You'll sleep like
tired little puppies.

YaaaawWWWwnnn.

"I'll say I love you like only a daddy can.

Good night, my little wild ones."